This

Angelina

book belongs to

. . . .

To my darling grandson, Max Dean, and his wonderful parents, Alexandra and Chris – KH

For Mary & Steve Inniss with love – HC

PUFFIN BOOKS
Published by the Penguin Group: London, New York, Australia, Canada, India, Ireland, New Zealand and South Africa
Penguin Books Ltd, Registered Offices: 80 Strand, London WC2R 0RL, England

puffinbooks.com

First published 2012
Published in this edition 2013

003

British Library Cataloguing in Publication Data
A CIP catalogue record for this book is available from the British Library

ISBN: 978–0–723–28143–6

To find out more about Angelina, visit her website at **angelinaballerina.com**

Angelina's Cinderella

Story by *Katharine Holabird* Illustrations by *Helen Craig*

PUFFIN

Miss Lilly's Ballet School was going on a dancing tour,
and Angelina was to dance as Cinderella. "It's my dream come true!"
Angelina told Alice as they hopped on to the little blue bus.
She waved goodbye to her parents.

"Good luck, Angelina!" they called back.

The little blue bus bumped along over hills and dales, followed
by Mr Nibbles in his tractor pulling all the scenery for the show.
The Cinderella Dance Tour was travelling all over Mouseland,
with a final grand performance at the famous Von Whiskers Castle.

No wonder all the little dancers were so excited – they'd been rehearsing dance steps and painting scenery for months! And now their great adventure was about to begin . . .

The mouselings' first performance was in Great Gouda. When they arrived, there was no time to rest. Mr Nibbles needed help to unload the scenery and set up the show.

And then Miss Lilly said, "Don't forget our dress rehearsal! Remember, dancers must practise every day."

By the time the rehearsal was over, Angelina's toes were sore and her pink ribbons were drooping.

"I'm so tired my tail forgot to twirl," she said, and fell fast asleep with her tutu on.

But the next day Angelina was all ready for her first show and happily danced onstage as Cinderella. She twirled about like a real ballerina even when Henry forgot to do his leap and Alice tripped over her ribbons. At the end of the show, the mouselings took a bow and raced offstage while the audience cheered. "Dancing is the best fun ever!" said Angelina.

Then it was time to pack up and climb into the little blue bus again.

"I absolutely love touring," said Angelina dreamily,
but Henry shook his head.

"Touring gives me a tummy ache," he said.

"Don't worry, my darlinks," said Miss Lilly kindly.
"You'll soon get used to it – all dancers do!"

When the Cinderella Dance Tour arrived at the Old Stilton Theatre Alice couldn't find her fairy wand and Henry was so homesick he didn't want to dance.

"I don't like this adventure any more," he said.

Angelina comforted him. "Don't give up, Henry. You're the best mouseling coachman ever!"

But later that night in her lumpy bed, Angelina couldn't stop thinking about her mother's lovely Cheddar cheese pies in the warm kitchen at home.

"Oh dear, I think I might be a little homesick too," she thought to herself before she fell asleep.

Every day there was more travelling in the little blue bus and another show. "I'm so very proud of my wonderful dancers," said Miss Lilly. "Everyone in Mouseland has heard about our fabulous Cinderella tour."

"It's so much fun dancing every day," Angelina told Henry,
"and I can't wait for our last performance at the castle."

"And I can't wait to go home!" said Henry.

At last, after bumpety-bumping all across Mouseland,
the little blue bus turned towards the grand Von Whiskers Castle.

Suddenly there was a loud thunderclap that made the mouselings jump, and the skies began to pour with rain. As the little blue bus raced towards the castle, Mr Nibbles's trailer got stuck in a deep, muddy hole.

"Oh, no!" cried the mouselings. And they all watched as their beautiful scenery toppled and fell into the mud.

"What will we do?" wailed Angelina to Miss Lilly. "Now we don't have any scenery for our final show!"

"Oh dear, what a mess," sighed Miss Lilly. "But I'm sure my clever mouselings will find a way. Remember, whatever happens, the show must go on!"

When Miss Lilly and the wet little mouselings finally arrived at the castle, Countess Von Whiskers invited them in for hot chocolate so they could all warm up. Angelina tearfully told the countess about the lost scenery. "We have to save the show," she said. "But what can we do?"

"Well, you might find something useful in the castle gardens," suggested the countess.

"Stupendous!" Angelina agreed. "Cinderella's fairy godmother made a magical coach from a pumpkin, and we'll make something magical from your garden!"

The next day the sun was shining again. "Come on, everyone, we're going to make new scenery!" Angelina announced at breakfast. All the mouselings happily followed Angelina and the countess to the gardens. "We can use flowers and plants," said Angelina. "Yippee!" shouted the mouselings.

They all worked together busily, making props and sets for the show.

Henry was very pleased with himself, because he came up
with a great idea for the coachman's carriage, while Alice
made a flowery fairy wand.

That evening, Angelina danced as Cinderella under the stars in the castle gardens. Everyone agreed it was a beautiful grand finale to the mouselings' Cinderella Dance Tour.

Alice twirled perfectly with her new fairy wand, and Henry was ever so proud of his splendid carriage. "What a triumph!" cried the countess, and she made Angelina and all the other mouselings promise to come back again next year.

At last the Cinderella tour was over and everyone felt a little sad.
It had been lots of fun – but they were glad to be going home.
"I like being on tour," said Henry sleepily. "Can we do another
one soon?"

But Angelina was already fast asleep on the little blue bus,
bumpety-bumping all the way home.